VANISHED
in Manhattan

MATILDA MARTEL

Gala

Everyone thinks I'm a good daughter. For eighteen years, I've played the part, swallowed my anger, and kept silent. My parents believe I'm crazy enough to marry that madman, Divo Talerico. They're mistaken.

Behind the scenes, I've made plans, saved every penny, and prayed everything will fall into place. The day before my wedding, I make my escape and finally see the light at the end of the tunnel.

Then he appears. My father's greatest rival, the wolf of Manhattan, Enzo Lupo, comes out of the shadows and kidnaps me.

He says he loves me but keeps me a captive in his gilded cage. He's beautiful, ruthless and his kisses make me feel things I've never felt before. But I won't run from one prison into another. I'll bide my time, make him trust me, and run again.

No cage can hold me.

Enzo

Manhattan is mine. In this city's underworld, everyone kneels to me. I've worked hard to build my reputation with bullets and blood, and yet, it's never enough. Everywhere I look, people want to take what's mine. I've devoted my life to building what my father started and keeping the power we've rightfully won. I spend so much time protecting my territory, I've given up the things we Sicilians cherish most, *family*.

My life is too dangerous to drag a good woman into my world, and I vowed long ago I wouldn't show weakness to anyone.

Or so I thought.

No one is more off-limits than Gala Lombardo. She's too young and meant for another man. But I can't help myself. Those big blue eyes, sharp curves, and full cherry lips were placed in this world for me, and I'll be damned if I let another man take what belongs to me.

In a moment of love and lunacy, I steal her away in the night and trigger a war that could ruin me for good. Bring it on. I'll destroy my enemies and make Gala the Queen of Manhattan. With her by my side, I'll rule the world.

If only she'd love me.

CHAPTER 1
GALA

All eyes fall on him. Enzo Lupo, the wolf, the don of dons, glides into the ballroom like we've gathered here for him. On cue, hushed whispers replace the boisterous laughter that filled this space only moments ago. The bride and groom bow their heads in reverence, honored by his presence, however late it may be. The band stumbles to an early finish and leaves the few people left dancing in a state of confusion. When they finally look towards the door, they scatter like rats and pray they haven't caused offense.

Lupo's steely gaze shifts from side to side, surveying his subjects like a feudal lord. I hold my breath like the crowd around me and wait for his next move. He typically shows his face and leaves, too busy to fraternize with the common people. And we prefer it that way.

It's scarier when he stays.

While we wait with bated breath, he looks over his shoulder and whispers to one of his men. After a few nods pass between them, the husky man hands him a white envelope, and he tucks it into his jacket. He turns to face the crowd and spots the wedding couple cowering near the front. Everyone invites him. You don't snub Don Lupo, leader of the

Five Families. But it's clear they never expected him to make an appearance. I have a hunch they would have spent more on catering, doubled the wine budget, and hired his favorite band. Two hours into this boring reception, I'm not sure there's anything left for him to eat. Such a ridiculous faux pas has been known to start wars.

He steps onto the marble floor. I place my hand over my mouth to quiet my gasp, stunned he's decided to stay. The rhythmic tap of heavy footfalls echoes across the room as one by one, a gang of thick-necked, broad-shouldered, heavy-framed men dressed in black suits and undoubtedly armed to the teeth follow Enzo onto the floor and head towards the bride and groom. They're hard to miss, but it's impossible to tear your eyes away from the figure at the front.

No one looks more dangerous than him.

He moves seamlessly, without hesitation or apprehension that he's the center of everyone's attention. He's used to people looking at him, and there must be a part of him that relishes it. He's dressed to impress and takes care of the way he looks. His navy blue Italian suit is perfectly molded to his tall, robust frame, snug on his waist and tight around his sculpted biceps. His chiseled jaw and cheekbones give his stern face an air of youthful beauty, like Michaelangelo's David but the gray hair dusting his temples remind you he's a man who's seen the world—a world you don't want to see for yourself. His gray-blue eyes are bright, piercing, and laser-focused, like an apex predator swimming through murky waters. Enzo Lupo is a Great White Shark swimming through a sea of guppies. Everyone here would love to take his place. Now I know why no one tries.

This is the closest I've ever been to him. I've spent most of my life sequestered from my father's life, tucked away at Catholic school, boarding school, or kept hidden at my grandmother's house in Yonkers. When I turned eighteen, my parents brought me back to prepare me for my wedding to

Divo Talerico, heir and number one enforcer for the Talerico dynasty. It's a loveless match. He doesn't want me any more than I want him, but people like us have no say in such matters.

We marry next week. I wish I could say I knew more details than that, but no one's bothered to consult me on any of it. Why would they? As far back as I can remember, I've been told my life isn't my own to command.

To my left, my father's pale face turn red, seething as he's forced to watch his greatest rival, a man twenty years his junior, claim the limelight he wanted for himself. For now, he plays the good soldier for fear anything less will cost him his life. But behind the scenes and in the shadows, I know he works to topple Lupo's kingdom and claim it for himself. It's a fool's errand. Nothing I've seen makes me believe he'll succeed. Lately, he can hardly afford to pay the household staff. I don't know how he believes he'll afford the muscle to take on Lupo's army.

While my father plots revenge, my mother has plans of her own---plans she hopes will restore our family's status and wealth. This rare appearance gives her the chance to show off her daughters and help them land the biggest fish in our waters. My eldest sister, Asia, discreetly lifts her boobs, smashing them into something resembling cleavage. My middle sister, Chiara, spritzes her pocket perfume, hoping she'll have the chance to introduce herself to the elusive bachelor. Most bosses Lupo's age would have a wife, a string of mistresses, and a house full of children, but they say Enzo is different.

He hates distractions.

Does that make him lonely? Someone like him doesn't need to be lonely. No doubt there are lines of women willing to keep his bed warm with no strings attached.

As soon as the thought enters my mind, I push it away with a quick shake of my head. My stomach sours, and a foul taste lingers in my mouth. I must be confused by the lure of the forbidden. It isn't his beauty I admire, although he has that in spades. I'm a naïve girl who's lived a sheltered life, and I have little exposure to men. One look at Enzo Lupo, and I can tell a dangerous animal is lurking deep beneath his calm veneer. And everyone knows wild things can't be tamed. They'll only turn on you when you least expect it.

Unlike my sisters, I have no desire to be with bad boys. I only long for their freedom. They get to do as they please and live by their own rules. If I could live like them, I'd run fast and far. No one would ever hear from me again.

And then I wouldn't have to marry Divo.

"Gala! Pay attention." In typical fashion, my mother's shrill snaps me out of my daydream and makes me jump out of my skin. "He's coming this way. Move towards the back, and don't try to upstage your sisters. You're already engaged." She twists my arms, digging her fingernails into my skin, and leads me into the crowd of gawking guests craning their necks to get a better look at the group of men headed our way.

"Stay put, please." She stuffs me between the wall and Mrs. Leone, the woman who grooms my sister's cat, leaving me in a state of befuddled amazement. I gather my billowy skirt and make room to cross my legs, smiling awkwardly as the kind old woman offers me some of her leftover cannoli.

I'm too embarrassed to look up and see the standing huddle part like the Red Sea. I dismiss the faint tap of footsteps as nothing more than the anxious clatter of high-heeled bridesmaids revving their engines. Someone clears their throat, but I ignore it. It can't be meant for me. I stare at the floor and crouch further in my seat, feeling confident I've made myself invisible behind Mrs. Leone's broad shoulders and ample bosom.

Only moments pass before a pair of Italian leather shoes

appear in my line of sight, and a smoky, silvery voice calls from above, "Are you hiding from me?"

I cringe with mortification and take a peek from under my lashes. Steel-blue eyes stare deep into my soul and hold me captive. The thumping beat of my heart quickens to a reckless pace, and my lips part, hoping to spill words that never appear. Shame brings me to my feet. Or perhaps it's the sheer force of his hypnotic gaze.

"I'm not..." A sudden rush of blood makes me sway in my shoes, and I instinctively place my hand on his chest to keep from falling. The sound of my mother's gasp makes me catch my mistake, and I tear my hand away, regretting I've taken such liberties.

"I'm sorry," I whisper, too frightened to say more.

He clasps my retreating hand and brings my knuckle to his lips. The air between us sizzles like a crackling live wire, and the skin on my arms prickles from the touch of his kiss. Tingles from a thousand butterflies fluttering in my belly travel down my legs and make me weak in the knees. If I wasn't scared out of my wits, I would find the strength to giggle like a nervous little girl. "They tell me your name is Gala."

I nod, then look from side to side, wondering who fed him this information. "Who are they?"

His perfectly chiseled features twist into a sinister grin. "We'll meet again."

We will?

CHAPTER 2
ENZO

THIS WAS SUPPOSED TO BE AN EXERCISE IN VANITY, NOTHING more. Whenever I receive an invitation to a wedding or christening, I prefer to make a brief appearance, deliver a gift and disappear into the shadows before anyone catches wind that I've arrived.

But I can't walk away tonight. With one glance, my heart set its course for life.

Gala Lombardo. I repeat her name, muttering softly and letting the syllables roll off my tongue as I set it to memory. It fits her perfectly.

I have a vague recollection of her existence. I'm sure I've heard her name in passing. But until tonight, I've never cast eyes on the other half of my soul. And that's who she is. I knew it the moment she came into view. Long dark waves of raven hair gleaming under the twinkling chandeliers made my head turn in her direction. A pair of pale blue eyes struck me down like a bolt of lightning, arresting the beat of my heart then jolting it back to life.

Of course, she's oblivious. Sitting between her sisters in a crowd of fawning guests, she has no clue our fates have just become irreversibly entwined. I was wrong to think I could forever command my heart. Control is nothing but an illusion. From this moment on, I cede the helm to destiny and follow her blindly to wherever she takes me.

And right now, she's leading me to Gala.

"What are you doing?" Bruno, my cousin, places his hand on my shoulder, fearing I've gone mad when I motion to my men that we'll be heading in.

I stare ahead and motion again, unaccustomed to having my orders questioned by anyone, even him. "We'll go in. Keep the twins with you at the front and then post two more men at each exit. The rest come with me. We'll give the bride and groom our well wishes, then I'll make the rounds before we depart. Aren't you the one who says I need to be more friendly?" I remind him of his recent accusation.

He frowns, probably wishing I'd chosen a classier event than the Russo-Marino wedding to become mister social. He's got a hot date with a hairstylist in Queens, and I've just put him behind schedule.

We all have a handful of critically defining moments in our lives. Sometimes a life-altering event comes down to a single last-minute decision that feels inconsequential when we make it. We turn right instead of left, take the stairs instead of the elevator, or simply walk through the wrong door. Coming here is one of mine. Bruno wanted to take the path of least resistance, send a courier with a hefty envelope of cash, and wash our hands of this whole affair. I chose to come.

I'd be an idiot not to see this through.

A chorus of gasps puts me on edge as we step into the hall. My shoulders stiffen, and I spot her in my periphery, watching me strut like a chimpanzee on parade, hoping to impress a female into mating. If she's Giovanni Lombardo's youngest daughter, she can't be more than twenty, making her sixteen years younger than me. That sounds terrible when I hear it in my mind. I'm halfway to the front, and it feels further than when we began. Beads of sweat line my forehead as the tension builds. I take a deep breath and suck in my abdomen, hoping to appear younger to the dark-haired girl staring slack-jawed at the far end of the room. I don't know what's come over me, but I need to rein this in before someone senses there's a chink in my armor.

I bring my eyes forward, tearing my lovesick gaze from the pair of plump red lips parted with curiosity at the strange man in the center of the room. I wish I could make everyone turn away and return to their cake. The bride should remain the center of attention. It's her day, not mine. In my desperation, I've done these people a disservice, but I'll make it up to them another day.

I quicken my pace in the final stretch and greet the couple with outstretched arms. They smile from ear to ear, but the fear in their eyes is unmistakable. I hand them an envelope full of hundreds, give them my heartfelt blessings and tell one of my capos to send them a case of my finest wines to make up for the intrusion. Their horror quickly subsides, and the band returns to playing the tarantella.

As guests file onto the dance floor, I lead my men into the rows of tables, greeting familiar faces with handshakes and hugs, on a secret mission to reach the girl in the mauve dress. While my bodyguards clear a path through a group of inappropriately dressed and over-perfumed women, I suddenly lose track of Gala. I twist my head from left to right, then crouch to see if she's taken a chair. In the distance, I spot a speck of mauve jammed against the wall and Mrs. Leone, a woman from my old neighborhood.

"Enzo, I didn't expect to see you here." Gio Lombardo approaches from my left and blocks my trajectory. With a look of obvious discomfort, he offers his hand. I despise his duplicity. He pretends we're friends for the sake of his survival, but he's living on borrowed time. I know he's plotting against me. My spies are planted everywhere—even in his house. It's only a matter of time before I catch him in the act. His connection to Gala may be the only thing that saves him.

"I'd like to meet your daughter." I don't wait for an answer but weave around his bloated body and head for the huddled girl pinned against the wall.

"Are you hiding from me?" We've never met, and it feels unlikely, but the timing is hard to dispute.

She tenses, lifts her gaze, and peeks coquettishly through a thick pair of lashes. The bluest blue eyes I've ever seen stare back at me, and my heart leaps out of my body, swiftly landing in the palm of her hand.

"I'm not..." The sweet sound of her voice sends a chill down my spine. I'll live to hear it always. I'll kill anyone who tries to silence it. When she rests her hand on my chest, I nearly pull her into my arms, but she backs away in fear. Her parents are close. She's not supposed to fraternize with someone my age. Especially, someone her father hates.

Before she slips away, I lift her hand to my lips and savor the scent of her skin. Our eyes meet and our lips part in a sigh, smothering words neither of us can speak.

"We'll meet again, Gala."

Something's begun tonight.

Something that will never end.

CHAPTER 3
ENZO

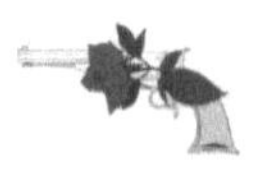

I like to think I'm in control, but everything in life has limitations.

Control and power are never permanent. I take nothing for granted and expect the unexpected. When a sudden case of chaos throws my world off-balance, I restore order swiftly. Perception is everything.

The men I command depend on my consistency. Ten years ago, I clawed my way to the top, and I've kept my reign by never losing sight of the vultures. Friends and enemies alike want to see me fall. They search high and low for any sign of weakness, so I choose to give them none.

Alcohol, drugs, women, pleasure, and various indulgences make a man weak, dull his senses and lead him to make bad decisions. I'm hardly a saint, but I know when to say when and I know when to stick to the plan.

A man in my position should be settled into a happy marriage with a house full of children. To a Sicilian, family means everything. Family comes before everything. In that sense, I've failed. I made a conscious decision long ago to spare my would-be wife from the life thrust upon me by my father. I denied myself of one of the greatest pleasures in life, but it gives me solace knowing I've prevented my children from carrying the burden I shouldered for years.

It isn't entirely selfless. Having a family makes me vulnerable to my enemies. Any worthy opponent knows if he kills me, he ends my suffering instantly. But if he goes after my family, he gets to rip my heart out every day for the rest of my life.

No amount of reward is worth that kind of risk.

At least, that's what I believed.

Gala would be worth it. I'd move heaven and earth to keep her safe if I could come home to those pale blue eyes alive with love for me and me alone. If I could fill my nights with Gala, making love a thousand times and a thousand ways, never tiring of one another until the end of time.

But she's so young---younger than I imagined. What kind of man would drag a young girl, a woman half his age, into danger if he wasn't one hundred percent certain he could guarantee her safety? I'd never forgive myself if she paid the ultimate price for my desire. Perhaps, it's best to leave well enough alone. She's eighteen and probably just started college. As much as it pains me to keep my distance, I'll keep an eye out for her. In a few years, when she's a bit older, and all this business with the Lombardos and Talericos has settled down, I'll pay her a visit.

My beautiful doll deserves to live in a peaceful world, and before I make her mine, I'll make it my mission to offer an olive branch to my enemies. A man should make himself worthy of the woman he loves. *Loves?* My heart thumps with confirmation, and I nod in agreement. I swallow hard, knowing my lofty plans are easier said than done. The mere suggestion elevates my pulse with rage.

"What are you waiting for? I don't pay you to stare into space and waste my time. I gave you all night to find out as much as you could about Gala Lombardo, and you've sat here boring me with idle chitchat about your mother-in-law. She's a nice lady, but she's not the lady I'm interested in." I stare at the long line of cars idling bumper to bumper two blocks from my office in Tribeca and cast an annoying glance at Angelo, the man I pay handsomely to advise me. The man currently annoying me.

He dithers, searching his mind for the proper answer and scouring the depths of his soul for the courage to tell me something I obviously do not want to hear. I can't believe I've retained this fool for so long. But his father worked for mine, and I'm loyal to a fault. The Marinos have served the Lupo family for generations.

"Bruno is right about her age. Gala turned eighteen this past July. She isn't a minor, as someone may have suggested." Angelo's gaze shifts from me to Bruno, waiting for us to contribute something to his statement.

"Yes, you were the one who suggested that," Bruno hisses, reminding him of an earlier argument. "She's my kid brother's age. They were in the same class at Saint Theresa's back in the day. But where the hell have they been keeping her? I haven't seen her in years."

"Stop talking, Bruno," I interrupt and point to Angelo. "Speak, or I'll kill you."

Angelo's shoulders slump, and he clasps his hands tightly in his lap. "Enzo, you're going to become angry, and you know how you get."

I roll my neck, cracking it one way and then the other. It's a nervous tick, but people always assume I'm getting ready for a fight. In this case, it's a little of both. Frustrated with his delay, I grit my teeth and groan, loosening my tie as my temperature climbs and sweat drips down my temples. "How...exactly...do I get?" My voice trembles as my smothered fury simmers.

Bruno nudges me with his elbow. "He means you sometimes don't distinguish between the message and the messenger."

Nonsense. I know the difference. But for the sake of moving this discussion along, I won't argue. "Angelo, out with it. I asked you to get the information. I know you can't control what you've been told." I breathe in, exhale and try to calm the beat of my racing heart. But if he doesn't tell me in the next thirty seconds, I'm going to grab him by the collar and toss him into moving traffic.

"All right." He holds out his hands and uses them as a shield. "I've made some inquiries and verified with several sources that Gala is engaged to marry Divo Talerico. They're getting married this Saturday at Saint Catherine's. In fact, it's been arranged for years. After the arrangement, they moved her to Westchester to live with her nonna, hoping to keep her out of trouble. I think that was Don Talerico's idea. She's such a beautiful girl. He didn't want her getting into any trouble before she married his son, if you know what I mean."

"Any trouble?"

"He means with boys," Bruno states the obvious and makes my hair stand on end.

My mind travels back to her face and the look in her eyes when she placed her hand over my heart. In that brief moment, I found my place in this world. My place is by her side. Her life and mine intersected at this very moment in time for a reason, and I won't blow this chance.

This news changes everything. If I wait, she'll be another man's wife, and as much as I believe she and I are meant to be together, some things are sacred. Gala. My Gala and Divo--that idiot, I mumble under my breath. Terror rips through my soul as I imagine my beautiful girl trapped in a loveless marriage, forced to surrender her body to his loathsome urges. I won't allow it. Her gorgeous body is meant for my filthy desires, not his. How can I stand by and watch her give him babies? That would finish me off quicker than a bullet.

"Are you okay, Enzo?" Bruno taps my shoe with his, then

points to my white-knuckled clenched fists sitting perched on my knees.

My mind snaps like a twig, and profound clarity visits me with a vengeance. "Where the hell do we find Divo?"

Bruno's eyebrows crease with confusion. "Divo? Are you going to kill Divo? He's Dante's son. Are you sure..."

My icy glare makes him cut his words. Angelo scoots forward, stuttering words that don't make sense before he slips into Italian, and he tries to talk me off the ledge. When I've heard enough, I hold my palm out to silence him. "I'm not going to kill anyone. Not today, anyway. I just need to talk to Divo. What do we know about him? Does he want this arrangement?"

Angelo shakes his head and leans back in his seat, relieved I'm not suggesting we put a hit out on a made man. "No, not at all. He's got a girlfriend, some high-society bird on Park Avenue he's crazy about. He's got no interest in Gala and only visits her when his parents make him. His old man is making him go through with it, but who knows if he'll even show up to the church."

I groan and sit in silence, ruminating on the best possible way to handle this without blowing everything to shit. I can't depend on maybes or assumptions about Divo's irresponsible nature. This is too important to leave to chance. There's no way I'll allow Gala to walk down an aisle until I'm on the other end.

As the car slows and drifts onto the curb, I push open the door and step out, hardly giving my driver time to shift into park. Time is running out to safeguard my future from this catastrophe.

"Bruno, take the Toscano twins and pay Divo a visit. Bring him to me. Dante isn't in the best of health. Divo will be the head of his family in a few years, and I know he's not as stubborn as his father. He wants to make money, and families who cooperate with me, make money. Giovanni Lombardo is bankrupt, and the Talericos will be soon. Divo will listen to reason. I'll make him listen." I weave past the doorman and head into my building. More than half of my business is legitimate and housed in a fifteen-story building near Rockefeller Park, a stone's throw from the Hudson River. We've been here since I took over, and I've turned my father's kingdom into a thriving empire.

Gala will be my queen---my empress. You don't steal a man's greatest treasure from right under his nose. I haven't come this far to let someone take what belongs to me.

Bruno takes his orders and heads back to the car. Angelo follows me into the elevator, so riddled with anxiety, he holds his briefcase to his chest and pants, "What do you plan to do with Divo?"

"Whatever is necessary."

CHAPTER 4
GALA

a child." My mother pinches my arm then hovers over the dressmaker's shoulder, giving her pointers about something she knows nothing about. Her nit-picking has nothing to do with the dress. It's a beautiful confection of lace and silk, precisely what she wanted and the opposite of what I requested. I can tell by the deer in the headlights expression she's worn since we arrived that she's worried about the cost and wants to argue her way into a discount. Unfortunately for her, Mrs. Columbo won't be intimidated.

"Madame, take a seat," the diminutive woman mumbles through the pins in her mouth and gestures towards a set of chairs in the corner. My sister, Asia, taps the chair and urges my mother to leave me alone. "For heaven's sake, you're making her crazy. The dress is perfect."

"It's not perfect," my mother frowns, gritting her teeth as she flails her arms and stomps in circles. "It's costing us a fortune, and I want my money's worth." My marriage to Divo Talerico was supposed to bring her a financial windfall. My father made her believe this arrangement meant wealth and security. But he lied. He needs alliances, and he needs to start somewhere. With one week left to go, she finally realizes she's sold me to a family of con artists.

Mr. Talerico promised to pay for my dress. He sent us to the best dressmaker in Brooklyn because he wanted his son on the arm of a goddess---his words. If it were up to my mother, she would have gone retail. She wouldn't have reserved the most expensive hall or booked stretch limos for the entire Talerico clan while she drove a Mazda to her daughter's wedding.

Last week, when the bills came in, Talerico feigned igno-rance and informed my mother other wedding expenses had tapped him out. I'm not sure which costs he means since my parents have paid for most of this farce. Still, as much as she complains, it's hard for me to sympathize with her situation. Even now, stewing with righteous indignation, undoubtedly texting my father for the hundredth time to nag him about maxing out her credit card, she thinks nothing of my broken heart.

"Are you all right, sweetheart?" Mrs. Columbo pins my bodice, the one she's taken in twice in the last four months. "You're getting too thin. Most of my brides lose weight before the wedding. Some are so nervous or so happy they forget to eat. They want to look perfect for their big day." She spots an errant tear creeping down my cheek and hands me a tissue. "But these aren't happy tears?"

I shake my head once and turn to face the wall, discreetly wiping the tears that follow. I thought I could go through with this. Divo is young and handsome. I thought things would change when I moved home to New York. My warped schoolgirl brain, twisted by loneliness, conjured a romantic fairy tale where Divo swept me off my feet and fought to win my heart. It's so ridiculous, I could laugh. No, not laugh. All I want to do is cry. I'll never know love or happiness. My life is over.

In one week, my life is over.

"Gala! We need to talk." Panicked and vaguely familiar, a brash male voice joins two thundering bangs on the fitting room door. "Gala! I know you're in there." His desperation and fear are palpable.

Who knows me? No one knows me well enough to seek me out.

"See who it is." Annoyed but never frazzled, Mrs. Columbo directs her assistant to the door and instructs her to get rid of the intruder. "She's in her dress, and we're not done yet."

"Gala!" Divo pushes through a crack in the door. Disheveled and bruised, he storms into the room looking like he's come from a fistfight. I can't believe I couldn't recognize his voice. But why would I? We've never spent more than a few minutes in each other's company. I'm stunned he knows which sister he's marrying, but I suppose the white dress gives me away.

"Divo! You can't see Gala in her wedding gown! It's bad luck." My mother and Mrs. Columbo block him like a pair of linebackers and stop in his tracks. It's only temporary. Their drive to preserve the rules of wedding etiquette is no match for his brute strength. He makes short work of their barricade by lifting Mrs. Columbo and setting her aside like a chess piece. "Gala," his voice softens as he approaches. "We need to speak. It's overdue."

"You're calling it off?" I stare into the bloodshot eyes of Divo Talerico, and my heart bursts with joy. This can't be real. How? Why? Details don't matter if this is true. "Can you? Will your father let you?" I stifle my smile, fearful my excitement will cause offense.

He nods, then shakes his head. "Come here." Divo spots my mother tiptoeing nearby and leads me into the hall. He takes my hand for the first time since our engagement, caressing it gently as we squeeze into a dressing room meant for one. This is the closest we've ever been, and I never want to be this close to him again. When he releases my hand, I wipe it against my dress, disgusted by his touch and wishing he was someone else.

"Why the sudden change? Will your father agree?" I need clarification. If I let hope enter my heart only to be disappointed, I may never recover. I'm too young to be so jaded. I don't want to give up on love so soon.

"Are you upset? Were you looking forward to the wedding?" He quirks an eyebrow, flattering himself at my expense.

My gaze narrows, stunned by his stupidity and vanity. "Of course not. I don't want to marry you any more than you want to marry me. What kind of husband would you make? You didn't even propose to me. Everyone knows you carry on with some prima donna socialite who likes to slum it with her bad boy Italian mobster. Who knows what kind of diseases you'll bring home to me, you jerk." I finally speak my piece, and I can tell by the look in his bruised eyes he wasn't expecting it. "What happened to you anyway?"

"You don't have to be so rude about it. I never wanted to marry you. You're eighteen years old. I've known you since you were six, and you'll always be a little girl to me. Everyone knows you're beautiful, but you just don't do it for me," he groans as he swims through waves of gathered tulle to find a tiny seat in the corner.

"You don't do it for me either." I cross my arms over my chest and give him my back. "But you still haven't told me how you're getting us out of this."

He sighs and stares at his face in the mirror. "I have no choice. I'll talk to my father tonight and make him understand. If we marry, our families lose support from Enzo Lupo. He'll cut us off at the knees and turn everyone against us. I've worked too hard for too long, fixing my father's petty shit, so he didn't flush our family's money down the drain. I can't afford to piss Lupo off. Look at what he did to my fucking face. And this was after I agreed to do what he asked!"

"Enzo Lupo did this to you? Why?"

CHAPTER 5
ENZO

"WHAT AM I HOLDING?" MY FINGERTIPS GRAZE THE EDGE OF THE card, unwilling to make full contact with the white invitation delicately embossed with Gala and Divo's full Christian names. Simmering with repressed rage on the verge of exploding, I place the card inches from Divo Talerico's hemorrhaging eyeballs and demand an explanation.

He tries to produce something resembling a smile, then shakes his head to assure me he isn't laughing at my expense. He reaches for it, then remembers his hands are bound. "It's not for the wedding. It's for tonight's rehearsal," he mumbles, spilling bloody saliva as he explains.

My eye twitches. There's something wrong with him. He's never been the brightest apple in the bunch, but his response stuns me. Maybe I punched him too hard, too many times. I make a mental note to stop hitting him on the head and change tactics.

"Divo." I motion to Bruno to hand me a chair then take a seat across from our prisoner. There's no way I can kill him. Not without consequences that would bite me in the ass. Divo and the Talericos are not worth those consequences. But he doesn't know that. "Did I or did I not tell you to cancel the wedding?"

He nods. "My father wouldn't let me. I swear I tried, but he threatened to disown me. Gala told me she's taking matters into her own hands. She plans to make a run for it during the rehearsal dinner, but she doesn't know her parents know all about it. They paid her cousin to spy on her. That's why I sent you the invitation. You said you wanted to help her, and tonight might be your only chance. I left a message with Bruno De Luca yesterday afternoon." He exhales and then rubs his bloody mouth against his shoulder.

My eyes flare with horror. I attacked him before he could speak and behaved like an animal. I unclench my fist and quickly untie him. The Toscano twins move in and help Divo to his feet, ushering him to the closest bathroom.

"Bruno!" I spin around and throw a right hook, striking him in the chin and knocking him on his ass. "Check your fucking messages!"

He plays possum--it's his typical ruse. Rather than face the music, he pretends to be out like a light. Curled up in the fetal position, his tense limbs give him away. When I tap my gun on his forehead, his eyes shoot wide open. "Do you have something to say for yourself? Where's your phone?"

"You didn't have to hit me, asshole." He rummages through his pockets and hands me his cell phone. I tap his birthdate into the password screen because, of course, he would have something so simple and scroll for Divo's number. "Eight unread messages, you prick. Eight unread messages. I've been waiting for information, and you've sat on eight messages and then allowed me to beat the crap out of him. You deserved more than one punch." I kick him while he's down and return to interrogate Divo.

There's so much more I need to know. The wedding rehearsal begins in five hours, and everything needs to be in place before then. If Gala's parents know she's planning to run, they'll have men planted outside the restaurant. I'll need to have my men take them out---or at least neutralize them until we can get her to safety.

"Divo, I need you to play along tonight. I'll reward you handsomely when you take over as don. Your father will never know you helped me." I offer my hand and feel genuine relief when he takes it. He's a much better man than I've been led to believe. He's just not good enough for Gala.

He nods and holds a bag of ice to his swollen face. "Will you go?"

"Only briefly, to pay my respects. I know that place well. The alley pulls up to the side exit, and there's room enough for a car. Whenever she heads to the restroom, the Toscanos will distract her cousin, and my men will be waiting by the exit. Is it Serafina? *It's Serafina, isn't it?*" I've shamelessly stalked my beautiful doll over the last week and noticed the buxom blonde develop a sudden interest in her much younger cousin over the past few days. It appeared odd at the time and now makes perfect sense.

"My father told me they promised her a job if she spied on Gala," he confirms.

"Can you distract her?" I turn to Michael and Matteo Toscano, my red-haired, blue-eyed, identical twin body-guards, well regarded in Little Italy as every woman's catnip, and watch their typical stoic expressions twist with discomfort. Hoping I'll change my mind, they give me a second to retract my request before their bodies slack with defeat.

"Fine," they groan with disgust, then nod in sync.

"Thank you. You'll be compensated for your troubles."

"We move at 6:00. Prepare my guest room for Gala Lombardo and send the priest from Saint Catherine's on an extended vacation just in case something falls through. I don't want to take any chances." I bark my orders and head downstairs to prepare for tonight. This act won't go unpunished, and there are no guarantees she'll love me.

But she'll be mine.

For now, that's enough.

CHAPTER 6
GALA

"Let me out! You have no right to keep me here!" I pound my fist against the door and feel the heavy wood thumping back against my tear-stained face. It's been close to an hour since someone pulled me into a car, put a bag over my head, and brought me here. *Where's here?* Nothing in this room gives me a clue.

"Please! Let me go! I won't tell anyone who you are! I didn't see your face!" I holler into the crack and plead for my release. It's not too late to run. If they let me go now, I can still leave town before the wedding.

I'd fooled my parents into believing I was okay and prepared to go through with this sham wedding. My bags were packed and planted behind the dumpster. My taxi was on its way. God helps those who help themselves. And I was done waiting for someone to save me.

Today, I quietly cashed out my savings and the two bonds my *nonno* bought me for my sixteenth birthday. Then I spent hours popping in and out of pawnshops, hoping to find the best offers for heirlooms I always believed I'd hand down to my daughters. As much as it hurt me to part with them, there was no time for sentimentality. Not with so much at stake.

Last night I prayed for a sign that I was making the right choice. I cried myself to sleep, clutching ancient baubles carried by my *nonna's nonna*, Apollonia Del Vecchio, through Ellis Island. She left the old country to escape an arranged marriage too. I felt her spirit was with me today when I made my escape. They could hunt me down and drag me back, but at least I'd know in my heart I tried. It was my final chance to be happy, and I had to take my shot.

Now everything is ruined. They'll ransom me to my parents, and I'll have to marry Divo. I'll have no choice.

I press my ear to the door and hear faint voices, then pounding footsteps pass in quick succession. They stop to discuss the girl-- me, they're talking about me-- but no one moves towards the door. I tap on the wood and call to the men, "Do you know who my father is? You'll have to answer to Gio Lombardo for taking me!" I kick the door and freeze when only raucous laughter greets my threat.

They're obviously aware of my family's diminished status. Then why take someone with nothing to offer? For a laugh?

I bang the door again, insulted I'm the butt of their joke, then jump away when the knob slowly turns.

"Gala?" A voice appears, and I know its owner the second the deep baritone registers in my ears. Gray-blue eyes emerge from behind the door, fixed in a smoldering gaze that sends my heart fluttering wildly. Fear and desire mix in an unfamiliar cocktail of lust, and I have a strange yearning to run just to see if he'd give me chase.

No, I'm furious and utterly appalled.

"Enzo...Mr. Lupo? What? Why did you? What am I doing here?!" I take a step back and clench my fists at my sides. His reputation is legendary, and there's little doubt he could kill me with his bare hands. But one way or another, I'm not going down without a fight.

"Divo asked me to help you. He was certain you needed help after discovering your cousin planned to betray you.

Would you like me to take you back to your parents?" He takes a step towards me and closes the gap I just widened. "I was under the impression you were trying to get away."

I shake my head then pause, recalling Serafina's peculiar behavior earlier today. "Do they know I'm here?"

"They only know you're gone. Taken by rivals. Your father's men were waiting for you outside the door. We dealt with them first. Please tell me if you'd like to return, Gala. I'll get you back at once. It's not too late to make it to Saint Catherine's by morning." One side of his mouth tilts into a mischievous smirk, and he takes another step towards me. I brace myself for his touch, something I've feared and craved in equal measure. He can't possibly imagine how often he's visited me in my dreams since our strange introduction last Saturday evening. And I prefer it that way. I'm done with this world and men like him.

"Just let me go. If you want to help me, let me go. Take me to the bus station, and I'll catch a bus out of town." I hiss, irked he's using my vulnerability against me and furious a part of me doesn't want to go anywhere. But I have to leave. This world is nothing but heartache. I won't be bullied or forced into what...what the hell does he want?

"You don't have to run. You're safe with me." He's so close. His voice vibrates off my skin and leaves gooseflesh in its wake. I cross my arms over my chest and hug my biceps, rubbing them feverishly for warmth, but it's completely unnecessary. The closer he gets, the hotter I feel.

"What do you know about what I need to do? Men like you do what you please. I decide nothing for myself," My voice stammers as his stunning blue eyes rake over my trembling body---from my tousled hair to my street-smudged pumps tapping nervously on the hardwood floor.

"You need to trust that I won't let anything bad happen to you, Gala. Can you trust me?" He takes my hand, and the fluttering sensation overwhelming my heart swims into my belly. My breath comes in pants as the scent of his mouthwatering cologne floats into my nostrils and marinates my brain with pheromones. Dizzying euphoria replaces common sense, and I whisper the words, "I trust you," without considering the man before me.

They say the devil has the power to assume the most pleasing forms. And his form definitely pleases me.

"What do you want with me? Why are you helping me?" I know the answer, but I need to hear the words from him.

"I want you."

"But what..." My mind blanks before I begin again. "What if I don't want you?" The lie pushes past my lips, and my eyes drift to the floor. I don't care if he knows I'm lying. My feelings are inconsequential. I need to leave before they're too big to control. I didn't escape one cage to wind up in another---however hot this jailor might be.

"Then you'll stay until you do. Get comfortable, Gala. You're not going anywhere."

CHAPTER 7
ENZO

DESPITE EVIDENCE TO THE CONTRARY, I CONSIDER MYSELF A patient man. This is not an adjective that anyone else would use to describe me, but I'd like to change that for Gala. My wife should see me at my best.

And she will be my wife.

I don't give a fuck if she doesn't know it yet. These kinds of things are set in stone by the angels. Talk to them, not me.

All right, I'm not a patient man, but I'm working on it. Three days in my house and she's hardly spoken a word. She asked for space, and I gave it to her. No more.

"Where is she?" I step off the treadmill and wipe a towel across my face. Michael Toscano hands me a bottle of water, and I chug it until it's drained. This is the second time today I've hit the gym. It's the only thing I can do to keep from going out of my mind or jacking off in the middle of the day. And I do enough of that at night. I don't want to play with myself---I want to play with Gala.

"She's in the pool, but she doesn't know how to swim, so she's just kind of standing there." Michael stifles a rare grin.

"She doesn't know how to swim?" My eyebrows furrow,

stunned but amused. Divo told me she didn't get out much, and that wasn't an exaggeration.

He smirks, "I guess no one ever gave her lessons."

"I guess someone should." I cross my arms and pull my t-shirt over my head. "I'll be around. Don't look for me."

The minute I walk in, I realize I've made a grave error in judgment. Michael wasn't wrong. My beautiful doll isn't swimming, but she's wearing a red string bikini that leaves absolutely nothing to my sex-starved imagination. My hungry eyes zoom in like telescopic lenses on the shape of her full breasts bobbing underwater. Her long legs skim the surface behind her as she pretends to glide, twisting and turning, unaware she's being ogled by a lecherous man rubbing his stiff erection at the door. If she sees me, so be it. She should know the kind of power she wields. I have a feeling she'll be brandishing it ruthlessly for the next forty years.

"Are you enjoying the water?" My voice breaks like a teenage boy during puberty. There's no limit to the depths I've sunk, and this is only the beginning. I rule over legions of made men, and this wisp of a girl has me tied up in knots begging for crumbs she doesn't know how to throw. I may hold the key to the door, but I'm the true captive here. I'm a thirty-six-year-old man in love with an eighteen-year-old girl. There's no way around it. I'm a dirty old man reliving my youth, and as far as I'm concerned, none of it matters. I need Gala, and I don't know how to make her mine without forcing her.

But that's unthinkable. Impossible. I'd sooner cut my dick off than force it on her. And a part of me still wants to believe she'll seek it out of her own free will.

"Are you coming in?" She stands erect, and her wet tits pop out of the water, jiggling without a care in the world and taunting my patience. I whimper silently when the ache in my balls catches me off guard, but I can't look away. Always a glutton for punishment, my eyes zero in on the red fabric molded tightly to her stiff nipples, and beads of cum drip freely from my angry cock. Is she doing this on purpose? Why would she? I'm the idiot who barged in on her private pool time.

"Are you okay?" She walks close to the edge and makes a sincere effort not to notice the bulge in my swim trunks.

I nod. *Maybe I nod.* I hardly remember running until I feel airborne cannonballing into the pool. Thankfully, she's smart enough to scoot away before I take her down in my wake. When I come up for air, her bright blue eyes meet mine, and I yank her into my arms, desperate to hold her. I'm thrilled when she doesn't pull away.

"Why don't you know how to swim?" I'm dying to kiss her. I think she wants to be kissed. But I can't put any faith in my overly active, psychotically obsessed imagination, and I won't push my luck so soon. *Gala will fall in love with me.* I knew it the moment I clapped eyes on her, and nothing could convince me otherwise. Falling head over heels in love with an eighteen-year-old girl is hardly ideal.

We don't choose who we love. Except right now, I can't imagine choosing anyone else.

"I was too scared to learn. I started lessons and almost drowned because the teacher wasn't paying attention. It traumatized me for years." She shrugs, pretending she's not embarrassed, but the flush on her face gives her away.

"I'll teach you if you want to learn." I shift our bodies towards the deep end of the pool and hold her tighter, gauging her response by resting my cheek on hers. I'm not sure what's going on, why she's suddenly speaking to me, but I don't want to question it.

"No, not today." She wrinkles her nose and wraps her legs around my back, letting me carry her weightless body through the water. "I heard someone say my father knows I'm here. Are you in trouble? Do I need to go back?"

"Did you decide to marry Divo after all?" I tilt my head

and drop my gaze to hers. "Is that why you're being nice to me? Are you trying to let me down easily?" I don't know her well enough to decipher her true feelings about the wedding. It's possible I've imagined our connection and projected my own desires onto her. She may have been running from Divo, but she never chose to run to me. Perhaps she believes he's the lesser of two evils.

Her water-logged lashes flutter before she closes her eyes and sinks her face into my shoulder. "No, but I don't want you to be in trouble over me. I don't want anyone to get hurt."

"What do you care? You said you don't want me." My response is harsher than I intended. She doesn't owe me a damn thing, but the longer I hold her in my arms, the quicker the madness drowns me.

"That doesn't mean I want you to get hurt." She brings her face inches from mine but keeps her lips out of reach. I loosen my grip on her waist and give her the chance to slip away. She doesn't take it.

"You won't get hurt, will you?" She smashes her breasts against my chest, raking her taut nipples against my skin. Adrenaline courses through my veins like quicksilver. Primal lust torments me.

I want to be patient, but I'm not a patient man.

"That depends..." I weave my fingers through her long hair and hold her head in place.

"On what?" she whispers, eyes wide, lips parted and less than a breath away from mine.

"On how much pain you plan to inflict..." Our lips crash in a fiery kiss that explodes as soon as its lit. Her mouth opens for me. My tongue pushes in, tasting, licking, swallowing each delicate whimper and inhaling the sweet taste of her breath.

"Gala..." I feast on her neck, then cup each mound of her supple breasts, caressing and pinching her nipples into stiff peaks that grow tighter between my teeth. I've lost my mind, but this is the most sublime madness I've ever felt.

"Enzo..." She purrs and climbs my body, practically stuffing her breasts in my mouth as we walk back into the wall, moaning, groaning, out of our minds in nothing more than minutes. I can tell by her inexperience she's never done this, and she wasn't planning this. Her enthusiasm surprised her as much as it did me.

"Let's get out of here," I say, lifting her out of the water but unwilling to dislodge her from my embrace.

She nods then freezes. "Oh no, wait. No, no, I better go." Gala unwraps her legs from my waist, grabs her towel from a lounge chair, and runs out the door.

I stare down at the enormous hard-on tenting my boxers and make an executive decision.

I should apologize and see if she's okay.

Then talk her into sex.

Maybe. Yes. No. *I'll play it by ear.*

CHAPTER 8
GALA

WHAT ON EARTH ARE YOU THINKING, GALA ADRIANA Lombardo? He's Enzo Lupo. The man kidnapped you and is currently holding you hostage in his seedy lair. It doesn't matter if it's an extravagant penthouse in Tribeca next to celebrities and Saudi princes. He's still a criminal holding you prisoner.

I wrap my towel tighter around my body, check both sides of the busy hall, then dart towards my room. Before I slip through my door, I look over my shoulder and check for Enzo. He didn't follow me.

Good. Is it good? *Yes, it is.*

I promised myself I'd be nice today. Three days of silent treatment haven't gotten me anywhere, and my *nonna* always said you catch more flies with sugar. If he trusts me, he'll give me the freedom to come and go. And he won't trust me unless he thinks I've fallen in love with him. When that day comes, I'll take my chance and run. I've still got my transferable bus ticket, and he didn't take the money I stashed in my purse's secret compartment. All is not lost.

My task was simple. If I bide my time and play his game, I can get back to my original plan.

Then Enzo kissed me, and my plan blew up in my face. Everything I ever wanted was right there in his arms---in his kiss. His soft lips, his tongue, the touch of his sharp teeth against my skin, and the taste of his hot breath made my body come alive. Lady hormones I didn't know existed took over my brain and made me do nasty things I wanted to do again and again. Oh my God, I want to do them right now!

If we'd gone somewhere else, if I'd let him take me to his room, I couldn't have stopped him. I would have pleaded with him to take it all---hard, fast, over and over until my voice was raw.

Look at what that man has done to me.

This is not the kind of sugar my nonna was talking about. And my plan will never work if Enzo Lupo makes me fall in love with him for real.

Oh my God, I can't believe I let him touch my boobs---with his mouth!

Wallowing in shame, I shuffle into the bathroom and flick on the shower. When I'm done, I'll ask the cook if I can eat dinner in my room tonight. I'm too vulnerable to face Enzo---and too horny. Those eyes, that body, even his voice gets my juices flowing. When you throw in the constant boners and my natural curiosity to finally see one in the flesh, you get a prescription for hot premarital sex followed by certain pregnancy.

And there's no time for those types of shenanigans. I have a bus to catch.

I step into the steam and let the hot water cascade over my cold limbs. It feels good---so much better than I deserve. I've defied my parents and spurned tradition. For three days, I've let them believe I was kidnapped by our enemies, Irish mobsters or Russian Bratva. For all I know, my mother could be crying her eyes out, having assumed I'm lying somewhere in a ditch, not getting felt up by a man twice my age in his penthouse pool.

Riddled with guilt, I add an extra dollop of bath gel to my loofah sponge, anxious to wipe away the evidence of my shame. It won't happen again. I'm not equipped to deal with a man like Enzo and walk away unscathed. Even now, his kisses haunt me, like a brand I can't remove from my skin. The movement of the sponge reminds me of his calloused hands. The water falling overhead feels like tiny licks lapping at my breasts. It only took seconds for him to imprint on my body, and no amount of water or soap could wash him away.

"Are you in there?" My ears perk at the sound of Enzo's voice, and his outline appears through the foggy glass---tall, ripped, and shirtless. This is too close for comfort. I'm naked, and he's almost certainly in need of a shower.

"Yes..." I shield myself under the water, fearing his side of the glass is more transparent than mine. "Didn't I lock my door?"

"It was unlocked," he blatantly lies. I know I locked it.

"But I checked it twice." I wipe a small window into the cloudy door to peep through.

He flashes a key, and a sly smile transforms his face. My heart flutters aimlessly as I feast my eyes on the man from my many dreams. "I want to see you. It didn't feel like we finished."

He makes no demands, but the look in his eyes commands my body like a maestro leading the philharmonic. Without a second thought, my wobbly legs step forward, and I push open the shower door, keeping no part of me from his view. When his gaze drops, taking me in from head to toe, I feel a slick dampness bloom between my thighs.

"*Cara mia*." He holds his hand to his chest. "You take my fucking breath away." He steps out of his boxers, and his steely cock bounces free, slapping his abdomen once before it juts out to full length. I suck in a quiet breath and sink my teeth into my bottom lip. My naïve gaze falls on the massive organ, and I clench my thighs, lost in lusty admiration.

"Enzo." I extend my hand, and he steps into the water. "I've never done this before."

"I know, sweetheart. I love you, Gala. I want you to love me. Whatever consequences I'll have to pay, I'll pay them. But you're mine, baby. You're fucking mine," Enzo growls into my ear, then hooks my leg over his hip. When he carries me into the wall, I put on the brakes.

"Wait, Enzo. Wait. I want to do this. I do. But I've never done anything before. Nothing at all," I whimper into his kiss and hold his chest back with my hand. "Today was my first kiss. Can we do this in degrees and not everything in one day?" Every word that squeaks out of my clenched throat feels like nails on a chalkboard. I don't want stages. I want Enzo, but the good girl still treading water somewhere inside me can't live with the knowledge that she had her first kiss and lost her virginity on the same day.

He nods with enthusiasm, turns off the water, and rushes us out of the shower. "Sweetheart, there are so many fucking things we can do. I'm about to blow your mind."

"Enzo!" My shivering limbs fall on the mattress, trembling with fear, need, and so much excitement I can hardly breathe. He cages me in, hovering over my naked body and surveying every inch like a predator moments from consuming his prey.

"Tell me when to stop. You only have to say the word. But you will have to say it because I won't be able to stop on my own." He spreads my legs, and my knees fly forward. I gasp with horror. Everything is on display. All my parts, all my wetness. He'll know all my secrets. I part my lips to slow him down, but his following words give me pause.

"Gala Lombardo, this is good enough to eat." Enzo dips his head between my thighs and takes a long, slow lick, separating the seam of my lady lips. He takes another and another. Lapping generously, gently, then brutally. When the tip of his thick tongue makes contact with my clit, I launch my hips into the air, and he catches my ass with his hands.

My screams build the rhythm. Each stroke gets me closer. The stronger the friction builds, the weaker I grow, the harder he tries. Enzo feasts on every ounce of my arousal, lapping juices he creates with every flick of his tongue before he stabs into my pussy to mine for more.

"Give me what's mine, Gala. We're not stopping until you come on my face." He curls a finger inside me, pumping in and out while his magical tongue assaults my bundle of nerves into trembling submission.

"You're so fucking tight, I can hardly fit two fingers inside this tiny pussy. We'll need to work extra hard to make my cock fit. You want that, don't you, doll? You want my big cock deep inside this little pussy?" He taunts me, filling my mind with visions that send shivers down my spine and straight into my core. I try to nod, assuring him I'll take whatever he wants to give, but words never form. I reach for the sheets, holding on as the world spins off its axis. My head rolls back. My muscles clench, seizing violently before everything slacks at once

"Enzo! Oh God, Enzo!" My pelvis bucks into his face as one spasm overtakes another. He's fucking magnificent.

"Let's make it last." He shifts to his knees and brings his cock to the apex of my thighs.

"Enzo…" I hold my hand out. "Not today."

"Trust me, doll." He runs his cock between my wet slit and bumps my clit. I jump and spur my ankles on his hips. He slides it, again and again, stroking my clit with the head of his cock and slapping my pussy with his heavy balls. I come again and again, lost in his kiss, entwined in his powerful arms, and hardly flinch when his hot cum lands between us.

Maybe I don't want to run away after all.

CHAPTER 9
ENZO

"G IO L OMBARDO KNOWS YOU HAVE HIS DAUGHTER, AND HE wants her back, Enzo." Angelo sits down in front of my desk, taps his forehead with a handkerchief then crosses and uncrosses his legs. He hates being the bearer of bad news, but where does his new information come from?

I've already dealt with my allies, and they've sworn neutrality. Yesterday, I secured promises from the Ivanov Bratva in Little Odessa to ignore the chatter. Rian Murphy, captain of the Irish mob in Brooklyn, has too many problems of his own to bother with mine. Divo needs to play his role of the angry, jilted fiancé, but everyone knows he's somewhere in upper Manhattan getting his rocks off with his favorite girl.

So, who has Angelo been talking to?

"I'm not worried," I dismiss his concerns with a wave and gesture for Matteo Toscano to come close. I hand him a note but keep the name on the envelope away from Angelo's view. "Why are you worried? Who's in your ear?"

He begins to backtrack, stammering and shifting in his seat. "I'm not alarmed about anyone seeking revenge. My wife is related to Gala's mother. They're second cousins. I only meant on a personal level. The Lombardos haven't seen their daughter in over a week and would like to know she's safe." He stares over my head, too frightened to look me in the eye.

I squint, narrowing my gaze with suspicion as I try to figure out his angle in all of this. The Lombardos have nothing to offer. They have no clear shot of unseating me on the best of days, and there haven't been good days in years. Angelo clearly loves his wife, but not enough to put his job and life on the line. "It's my understanding they went months without seeing their daughter when she lived with her grandmother. Why the sudden sentimentality? Do you have something to say, Angelo?" I remove my gun from its holster and place it on my desk.

He shakes his head and takes an audible gulp, "I'd never betray you, Enzo. I'm just trying to warn you. Your interest in Gala Lombardo has made her a target. With so much at stake, Gio fears you won't be able to keep her safe. He wants to send her to live with family in Italy."

My eyes nearly shoot out of my skull. Italy? Are they out of their fucking minds? Has Angelo lost his fucking marbles even suggesting it to me? I lift my gun and point it at his head. "What did you say?"

He clasps his hands, mocking prayer as he pleads for his life, "Don't shoot the messenger, Enzo. People are more upset than they'll admit. You've yet to state your intentions with Gala. She's eighteen years old, and it looks like you've turned her into your personal whore..."

I don't let him finish. I shoot past his head and nick the side of his ear, more than likely shattering his eardrum. He clutches his face, whining in pain over a graze.

"You don't talk that way about my future wife and the mother of my children." He watches me speak, but I'm almost sure he can't hear a word I'm saying. "Gala and I will marry as soon as the church allows us to have a real wedding. I'm not taking her to fucking city hall. Tell your wife to tell her cousin to stay the hell away from my Gala. If they lay a finger on her, they'll answer to me. If they try to take her, I'll kill them with my bare hands, and you better believe I'll take more than their ear." I fight the urge to kick him while he's down and holler for Bruno.

"What the hell happened here?" His befuddled expression feels rehearsed, but I push it out of my mind until I know more.

"Get him out of here. The twins are with me." I storm past my two closest advisors and take refuge with people I know I can trust.

Michael and Matteo follow close, hot on my heels as we head for the cars outside. "Tighten the security at the penthouse and watch Bruno. Matteo has my instructions. Angelo just informed me Gio wants to send Gala to Italy to keep her safe. It's bullshit. They don't know I know all her relatives live here." I take the stairs two steps at a time, then slide down the banister, eager to get to my car. "Fifty to one, that bastard wants to pawn her off to someone else in exchange for an alliance or who knows, maybe just to spite me." I fling open the car door and jump into the back seat.

"I need to get back to Gala."

CHAPTER 10
ENZO

THE WORDS REPEATEDLY CHURN IN MY MIND. GIO WANTS TO TAKE Gala to Italy. Over my dead, rotting, maggot-consumed corpse will I ever let him take her out of this country. And if he did, I'd hunt her down and bring her back.

Nothing would keep me from finding her.

Nothing will prevent me from keeping her safe.

But does Gala want to stay? For the past four days, we've humped like sexually repressed teenagers at prom---doing everything but the main event. I've told her I love her. She knows I'd do anything to keep her with me. I want her to stay of her own free will, but she also knows I won't let her go.

That makes no sense. I know it makes no sense, but neither does the ache in my soul that grows wider and deeper every day she keeps her heart hidden from me. So, she prefers me over Divo. I should be flattered, but I want more. I need her to look at me the way she looked at me the night we met. I should have taken her then. Or not at all.

But then she'd be another man's wife.

"Enzo, we can't find her." Three of my men meet me at the door, waving guns and barking orders into their headsets. One flies by me and darts into the stairwell while the other heads to the back of the house. The third stays behind to brief me.

"What do you mean you can't find her?!" I grab him by the lapels and shake him. "You're here in my house for the specific reason of watching Gala. That is the only thing I pay you to do." I rip the gun out of his hand and threaten to whip him with it.

He holds out his hands and shouts, "Not us. We were between shifts. He knew the exact time we changed shifts and came within those five minutes. He tied up the cook and locked the maids in the closets. They said he pretended to be a delivery person from a butcher shop that delivers every Thursday. The doorman out front said he was new, but he had the proper identification. He busted in and worked his way through, catching everyone by surprise. We shot him on his way to your bedroom, but we don't know if an accomplice took Gala. We can't find her." The desperate look in his eyes tells me he's turned the place upside down. I can't bear to ask another question.

I cock my gun and walk towards our bedroom. The heavy scent of Gala's rosemary shampoo lingers in the hallway. The musky aroma of our torturous foreplay still hangs in the air. My heart shatters, splintering into tiny pieces that pierce my soul and awaken the beast.

I storm through the hall and bark at the men filling the foyer. "Everyone get to the fucking street. Call the butcher and nail his ass to the wall. I want to know why someone had his uniform. Whoever it is had help from my organization. Get the Toscanos here now, and keep Bruno out of the loop." I shout my orders and reach for my phone. We need reinforcements, and I need information.

One missed message highlights the screen. It's from Gala.

I'm on the roof. Please come get me.

My brain explodes, and my feet move before I finish reading her message. I race to the end of the hall and climb the narrow staircase that leads to the roof. I hadn't been up here in years, but two days ago, I snuck Gala out for a bit of nighttime exhibitionism. Thank God for my perversions, or my doll might never have known where to hide.

"Gala!" I swing open the door and find her shivering in a corner, hunkered down on her haunches, and hugging her calves.

"Enzo! It was my father's man. I recognized him." She jumps to her feet and flies into my arms. I kiss both sides of her tear-stained face and lift her legs over my hips, rocking her gently to soothe her fears.

"I know, and he'll pay for it. You're mine, Gala. You're fucking mine. No one takes you from me. Get used to me, baby. Figure out how to love me and let me love you because I'm not going anywhere. Do you hear me?" I seal my lips to hers and hold her as close as two people can be while fully clothed. Except I don't want to be clothed. I want to be naked. I need to warm her up inside and out until we're both so hot we're liable to set this whole damn building on fire.

"I love you. But you know that already—don't you? You're so cocky, Enzo." She shakes her head and jabs her fist into my chest. "You knew you had me wrapped around your finger the first time we met. You didn't need to kidnap me. Why didn't you just ask me to run away with you?" She digs her face into my neck and points to the door. "Can we go inside? I'm freezing."

I deserve that.

"I am cocky, baby. I'm a cocky shit. That's why I talked to a priest yesterday without talking to you first. Don't hold it against me. I want to marry you. If you'll have me...please." I rush downstairs and kick open our bedroom door. "Will you?"

Gala climbs onto the bed and pulls off her sweater. Her long raven hair falls past her breasts, her blue eyes sparkle with mist, and her red lips swell into a tiny pout. My beautiful doll nods once and then proceeds to unbutton my shirt. "I'll have you." She unfastens her bra and tosses it on the floor.

I drop my pants and ease out of my boxers. My eyes travel over Gala's eighteen-year-old body---virginal, ripe, and entirely mine. I memorize every curve and angle, wanting to keep this photograph in my mind forever. It's not every day a man knows he's making love to his wife for the first time. "I promise I'll never let what happened today happen again. I'll always protect you."

"I trust you, Enzo."

"Good, because you're about to see a whole new side of me, sweetheart." I crawl onto the bed and slide my hand between her thighs. Dampness soaks my fingers, and I bring the familiar taste of her arousal to my mouth. "And trust is key."

Her puffy lips tilt up into a one-sided smirk. "You're such a cocky shit."

CHAPTER 11
GALA

HE SEARS HIS LIPS TO MINE, AND I KNOW IN MY HEART HE'S igniting a flame we'll never extinguish. I could leave. He trusts me, and after the heat dies down from today, he may let me come and go as I please. I could take my ticket and disappear to a safer world and never return to people like my father. But I'll never find another Enzo, and my heart would never recover from his loss.

His mouth moves down my jaw, and tiny tingles of anticipation dance across my skin. I want him more than I want air. I need to feel his weight on me, his cock pumping in and out, breaking, claiming, thrusting hard until I can't remember my name. Because after today, I never want to be a Lombardo again.

"I can't lose you, Gala." His hands follow the path through the valley of my breasts and stop to caress each mound of swollen flesh. He kneads gently, letting his fingers tease my nipples until his tongue replaces them. I twist in his arms, moaning and sputtering out of control when his hand cups my pussy and sinks into my moist heat. I'm so wet, with every pass of his hand, slickness drips onto my thighs.

"What a bad girl. Are you ready for me?" The sound of his

deep voice makes me hum with glee, and I nod like a child---eagerly and joyfully. I'm more than ready. I'm desperate for more, for him, a rougher touch, a friction that releases the tightly wound coil building within.

"Please, Enzo. Stop teasing me."

He licks the dampness off my thighs and twirls his tongue around my clit. He does it slowly, methodically, with the patience of a psychopath who wants to torment his victim. I greet his abuse with a quick succession of high-pitched squeals as I writhe and tremble, shamelessly gyrating my soaked pussy into his mouth.

"You teased me for days." He shoves two fingers inside me, and I spread my legs wider, hoping he'll give me what I want.

"Tell me what you want, Gala. I don't think I can go easy on this pussy." He pumps his fingers in and out, stretching me open and creating a tension that's only seconds from exploding. "I need to watch it swallow my cock whole." I gasp, feigning offense, but his nasty words inspire me.

"What do you think I want?" Now it's my turn to delay. I gyrate my hips, fucking his fingers, undulating my body around his hand like a pornographic puppet until I near the precipice of the divine plane. My breath hitches, once, twice, then every muscle tenses in a shuddering climax that hits me like a freight train.

"Enzooooo!" I hold his hand, needing a tiny reprieve as currents of unbridled ecstasy surge through me, shaking and seizing every limb until I'm nothing more than a sweaty collection of satisfied bones. Enzo doesn't hesitate a second more. He covers me with his body and hooks my trembling legs around his back.

"I love you," I scream the words just in time to feel the first inch go in. It glides in with ease. I'm so wet, I stretch open and take one inch, then two more, before my clenching walls struggle to fit his massive girth.

"We can go slower, sweetheart," He whispers through a Cheshire cat grin, pulls out, and runs his thick cock down my slit. He repeats the motion, sinking into my wetness, again and again, nudging my clit, rebuilding the rhythm of my climax until my body startles back to life.

"Please, Enzo. You won't hurt me." I stare transfixed at his chiseled body, salivating over every sculpted abdomen as he thrusts his hefty cock inch by inch, stretching and wrecking my pussy with the brutal intensity I craved since the moment we met. Loving him was never going to be sunshine and rainbows. He's a hard, dangerous man, an apex predator at the top of the food chain---and I want him to love me like one.

"Breathe, baby. Let me in. I love you more than God." His blasphemous words stun me into submission, then fuel the wickedness within. I tighten my legs around his hips and adjust my angle. Whimpering softly, I sink down, taking him in, letting him fill me until there's nothing between us.

"That's it, baby, take this big cock." He lifts my ass off the mattress and pummels his length to the hilt. "Fuck me back, Gala. Take what's yours, baby." My heart races, bursting with lusty joy as I bear down, rolling my hips to work him in, again and again, claiming the man I love as much as he's claiming me.

"I can't live without you," he groans, pumping brutally as he pushes my knees to my shoulders. His ruthless stride breaks and rebuilds me. Every thrust brings us closer to the unspoken goal. Pleasure grows, stroke by stroke. The harder he thrusts, the more I feel, the wetter I become. We were meant to be together, and what happens tonight could seal our fates forever.

"I was so scared I'd lose you. I couldn't survive it...not anymore." His sky blue eyes bore into mine and brand my thundering heart for good.

"You won't. I love you, Enzo. I won't leave you---not if I

can help it." I mean every word but need assurances of my own. "And you better not leave me!"

His lips seize mine. "Never, baby. I'd claw back from the dead to keep this tight pussy. You will never get rid of me." His meaty hands trap my breasts. My nails dig into his ass. He thrusts harder, ramming and rutting with purpose as our limbs twist and our bodies meld in a deep chasm of primal mating that sends us tumbling rudderless into sticky hot erotic bliss.

"Fuck! Enzo! I love you." I fall into a heap of sheets and let him slide me into his sweaty embrace.

"Was that cocky enough for you?"

He always has to have the last word.

CHAPTER 12
EPILOGUE-ENZO
EIGHT MONTHS LATER

Today, we clean house---in more ways than one.

"Oh, please don't sit there. The pillows! I've just finished plumping them into perfect little marshmallows, and I don't want you flattening them out like last time." Gala buzzes around me, refolding blankets, straightening photos, and rechecking the blinds for dust. She's nesting. The doctor said this is entirely normal third-trimester behavior, but today she's got it turned up to eleven.

"I didn't flatten anything. It was your fat cat." I point to the recent painting she commissioned and watch her confused expression turn peevish.

"Luigi weighs ten pounds. The vet swears that's ideal." She clutches her belly and gives me her back. Ever since her parents lost their home and her older sisters were forced to move into an apartment together, she's taken ownership of the family cat. It was supposed to be temporary, but four months in, and she refuses to hand him back.

"Where is he, anyway?" I search the floor and see no sign of him. Like the other male in this house, he's rarely far from Gala's heels.

"I had one of the guys take him to Mrs. Leone for his

grooming appointment. Asia and Chiara plan to stop by later today, and I don't want them to get any ideas about stealing him back. He'll be a big brother soon. He has responsibilities here." She rocks on the balls of her feet then spreads her arms for a hug.

I take a long look at the beautiful raven-haired girl in front of me, and my heart swells with pride. Gala Lombardo, no, Gala Lupo is mine. *I knew it.* My instincts are never wrong. The girl across the room stole my heart and washed away all my fears in a matter of seconds. Loving her never made me feel weak. I feel more powerful than ever. I'm ten feet tall with my beautiful doll by my side.

Seven months ago, I promised 'til death do we part. I couldn't give her the church wedding she deserved, but she wore a long white gown, and we threw a party in Vegas. It had to be done in secret, and it had to be done fast. Not only were we expecting our daughter, but we learned her father made a deal with my enemies in Italy---men who wanted to use Gala against me.

I had to protect what was mine. My girl first, then my kingdom.

Fortunately, I've retained both.

"Are you ready?" Michael Toscano appears at the door and offers Gala a kiss on the cheek. After everything that went down, the twins were officially promoted to capos. I trust them with my life, and more importantly, I trust them with Gala's.

As it turns out, my suspicions were right about Bruno. As soon as he saw a chink in my armor, he thought he could pounce and unseat me as boss. Together with Angelo, he believed he could send me over the cliff by selling Gala to my enemies. I'd lose my mind, go on a killing spree, and be ousted from my position. As the underboss, he'd take over.

To my horror, Gio Lombardo was a willing participant. His ambition and hate for me eclipsed his love for his own daughter. I tried to keep that from Gala for as long as I could. But she found out on her own and cut her father out of her life.

The Toscanos gathered the evidence and helped me catch Bruno, Gio, and their accomplices red-handed. Some are still with us, exiled to Italy, and some have been dealt with in ways I'd rather not discuss. Gio is alive because I won't kill my wife's father. But I have little doubt someone else will eventually finish the job.

The last man standing is Dante Talerico, Divo's old man. But today, his time is up. He's held onto power and dodged the consequences of his defiance for far too long. No more. Today, we give him a choice to step down and name Divo as the new don or lose everything. He'll put up a fight. He may even storm out. But he'll listen to reason because he's not a fool.

Divo deserves to be don. As much as I hate to admit it, he was instrumental in my good fortune. Plus, he endured multiple beatings that I still feel slightly terrible about.

"I'm ready." I amble towards Gala, still busying herself with organizing her collection of snow globes, and snake my arms around her belly. She wiggles into me, rubbing her ass into my twitching cock, suddenly awake from a jolt of Gala's pheromones.

"When will you be back?" She flutters her lashes and smooths my hands over her bump.

"Cut that out. You know that gets me hard. I can't go to this meeting thinking about last night." I shield her from Michael's view and discreetly knead her giant breasts. Her happy hormones have returned with a vengeance, and I only have six more weeks to indulge in my fiendish love for pregnancy sex.

"You were magnificent." She turns her head onto her shoulder and whispers. "You almost sent me into labor, Enzo Lupo."

My cock climbs to full mast. I thread my fingers into her dark hair and pull her back for a kiss. "I'll be back in three hours. Be ready. Be wet. I'll call the maternity ward and tell them to expect you."

THANKS FOR READING!

For more of Divo's story, look for SECRET WEAPON,
    Preorder Now, Releasing May 20

VANISHED SERIES

Captivated by their captives, these made men only answer to the women they love.

Dangerous bad boys, thrilling suspense, and passion worth dying for. These possessive men will break all the rules to claim the women who have stolen their hearts.

If you love boundary-pushing men who are sexy, scintillating, and seriously dangerous, this is the series for you.

Vanished in Brooklyn by Kylie Marcus

Vanished in Boston by Ava Pearl

Vanished in Chicago by ChaShiree M.

Vanished in Atlanta by And Lynn

Vanished in Nashville by Sammy Starlight

Vanished in Cleveland by Rebecca Gallo

Vanished in Manhattan by Matilda Martel

Vanished in Baltimore by Alana Winters

Vanished in Denver by Layne Daniels

Vanished in Vegas by S.E. Isaac

Vanished in Newark by MK Moore

And order the entire Vanished Series here

ALSO BY MATILDA MARTEL

If you'd like to read more about Divo Talerico,

Preorder Secret Weapon now!

Releases May 20, 2022!

DO YOU LOVE STEAMY AGE GAP ROMANCE?

Those are my favorites.

If you like them as much as me,

you might like these titles:

My Second Chance

Takeover

Blindsided

Get Your Kicks

The Pastor

In Praise of Older Men

My Heart's Desire

Maestro

Gilded Cage

Love Match

Play Right

The Man I Love

Bad Boss

Clever Girl

Chasing Zoe

The Good Girl

My Ward

Do you love Billionaire Romances?

Try these titles:

Takeover

Filthy Rich

Filthy Love

Blindsided

Gilded Cage

Magic Man

Hostile Takeover

There She Goes

Agreeably Arranged

Bad Boy

Do you love Friends to Lovers?

Shut Up & Kiss Me

Unsuitable

Lucky Man

Marry Me

Do you love Mafia Romances?

Check out my BROOKLYN BAD BOYS

Love Interrupted

Love Unleashed

Love Revealed

BAD BOYS TURNED GOOD?

Check out SCOUNDRELS IN LOVE

Bad Professor

Bad Boss

Bad Boy

PHILLY BOYS FIND LOVE IN LOVE BITES

Love Hate

Love Nest

Love Match

And many more - find them HERE

Thanks for reading and I hope you come back again!

ABOUT THE AUTHOR

Matilda is a Texas girl in love with a Philly boy who loves to write dirty books about two people who trip into love and fumble their way into a Filthy, Funny, Happily Ever After.

I live in Austin, with my husband, two crazy Chihuahuas and an even crazier cat. And I spend most of my day writing dirty romance books about older men who fall in love with younger women and make fools of themselves trying to win their hearts.

If you love Dark Romance, you've come to the wrong place. I don't like dark heroes.

I like my hero to be successful, sweet, suave, sophisticated and kind--- and then I want him to lose all his composure and game when he meets the heroine. I want him to turn into a bumbling idiot when he spots the girl of his dreams and revert to a teenage boy in a man's body trying to win her.

I like my heroines to be witty, intelligent, and unshakeable---who could do just as well without a man—until the hero convinces her otherwise.

I write A LOT OF AGE GAP--because I LOVE AGE GAP ROMANCE. I've got no other excuse for it.

No matter what kind of story it is, my ladies are ADORED, and my endings are always Happily EVER AFTER, not HFN.

To receive a free ebook, join Matilda Martel's newsletter.

Please head to my website to learn what's in the final stages and will be coming out soon!